Captain Confidence Saves the Day

Printed in the United States by
GCG Publishing
Chesterfield, Missouri 63005

Dedication

I want to dedicate this book to Jerry and Geneva Archable, my mom and dad, who sprinkled the seeds of confidence in me. They told me at an early age that I can do anything I set my mind to.

Kaelynn Gore, my beautiful daughter
I live for you. My every thought is to make a better life for you. You are a blessing, and your self-confidence will allow you to fulfill all your dreams. I want you to carry on the legacy of remaining confident in yourself first and sprinkling the seeds of confidence in others. I love you with all my heart, Poo.

LaMorra Shonta Davis-Archable
My beautiful wife, you are a true blessing. Thank you for listening to and supporting all my ideas. Thank you for seeing my vision. Thank you for loving me as is. I will give you the world.

Georgia Mae Dunn
My beautiful auntie, I miss you dearly. You were my number-one supporter. Thank you for showing me unconditional love.

Bernice Halbert
My beautiful grandmother, you showed me strength. I will never forget the sacrifice you made when you were sick. I am forever grateful for the gift you gave me—that is, my mother, Geneva Archable.

ACKNOWLEDGMENTS

The completion of my first book could not have been possible without the participation of so many people whose names may not all be listed.

I would like to express my deep appreciation and indebtedness particularly to the following:

To God
To PHI Chapter and Alpha Psi Kappa Fraternity, Inc
To Koran Bolden, who spoke life into my vision and dream
To all relatives, friends, and others who shared their support

Thank You

Classroom

Kaelynn is a five-year-old girl starting kindergarten today. She is looking in the mirror with sadness. As she does so, she begins to cry. "I hate the first day of school." Her mom comes into the room and sees her crying. "What's wrong?" "I hate the first day of school," Kaelynn says. "Why?" her mom asks.
"I don't know anyone, and I don't have any friends, and I might have to introduce myself."

Her mom assures her she will be fine and will make friends. "When it's time to get in front of the class, take a deep breath, and say your name is Kaelynn."
Kaelynn begins to cry harder. Her mom is shocked because she thinks she had given her words of encouragement.

After dropping Kaelynn off at school, her mom sits in her car for a moment and looks up to the sky. "All my daughter needs is a little self-confidence to get through the day."

Kaelynn enters the school with her head down and is greeted by Ms. Davis, who is her teacher. Kaelynn looks up with a slight smile and says, "Hi." Ms. Davis welcomes her to her class and tells her to sit wherever she chooses. Kaelynn backs up and starts to cry because there is only one seat left in the front of the class. Ms. Davis directs her to the seat, and Kaelynn sits down, fearful.

After Ms. Davis introduces herself to the class, her next statement horrifies Kaelynn. "Now, class, I want each of you to come to the front of the class and introduce yourself and tell the class something funny about yourself." Kaelynn starts to tremble.

As Captain Confidence is flying over the world, he has a feeling that someone needs him in Saint Louis, Missouri. He flies to Kaelynn's school and lands on the roof. He knows that Ms. Davis is about to call on Kaelynn to introduce herself.

Captain Confidence's mission is to sprinkle the seeds of confidence to empower people to have no fear and to believe they can do all things. He sprinkles these seeds on Kaelynn's classroom.

As Ms. Davis motions for Kaelynn to get up, Kaelynn feels a burst of confidence. She stands in front of the class. "Hi, my name is Kaelynn Priscilla. I am five years old. I like french fries, and something funny about me is I like candy." Her smile is huge, and she continues to stand in front of the class. Her classmates begin to cheer and clap and say, "Good job." As Kaelynn heads back to her seat, she cannot stop smiling.

The rest of Kaelynn's day is fantastic. Captain Confidence sees her run to her mom's car at the end of the day.

Kaelynn gets into the car. "This was the best day of my life."

Her mom looks surprised. "Really?"

Kaelynn tells her mom about her introduction to the class and how she got a burst of self-confidence.

Her mom looks out the window and into the sky. "I asked for self-confidence for my daughter, and she received it. It's like a superhero heard my request." Yes, Captain Confidence saves the day.

Trenton

Trenton is in middle school and contemplating trying out for the school basketball team. He has always wanted to play but doesn't think he is good enough. The tryouts are tomorrow. Trenton has practiced throughout the summer and went to a basketball summer camp. He is confident playing in the backyard but feels he is not ready to play for a team.

The next day, Trenton wakes up with a stomach ache and tells his mom he is not able to go to school. Trenton's mom knows he is nervous about the basketball tryouts, so she hugs him and tells him he will make the team but has to have confidence in himself. Trenton's stomach starts to hurt more. His mom gives him some medicine and a kiss on the cheek. She smiles. "Trenton, get ready for school, because you are going to school."

At the end of the day, the school bell rings. Trenton heads to the locker room, and the stomach pain comes back. As he laces up his lucky sneakers, he begins to think about all the reasons he shouldn't make the team.

As Captain Confidence is flying over the world, he gets the feeling of low self-esteem coming from someone in the gym of Trenton's school. Captain Confidence quickly flies there and peers into the gym window.

Captain Confidence sees Trenton sitting on the bench, nervous. The coach signals for Trenton to start basketball drills. As Trenton starts to walk to the basketball court, Captain Confidence flies in and sprinkles the seeds of confidence on him.

Trenton grabs the basketball, shoots, and makes a basket. He gets the ball again, shoots, and makes another basket. He uses his skills to dribble through his legs and shows his ball-handling moves. The coach's mouth drops open in surprise, and his eyes are fixated on Trenton. The coach blows his whistle and stops the tryouts. He waves Trenton over. "You have to be on the team. You made the team."

Trenton looks in disbelief, and Captain Confidence smiles as he flies away from the school. After tryouts, Trenton rushes to his mom and dad, who are waiting in the car. "I made the basketball team!" Trenton says.

His parents smile. "We knew you would make it," his mom says.

"You just have to have self-confidence, Son, because confidence is everything," his dad says.

Again, Captain Confidence saves the day.

Bullying

Twins Kayden and Tayden are brother-and-sister twins who hate going to school. Every day as they are walking to school, one of the middle schoolers waits for them at the corner and makes fun of them because they are twins.

Kayden and Tayden have tried to take a different route, but it makes them late to school. Kayden feels he has to protect his sister from the big bully, but he is scared the bully might hurt him.
As Captain Confidence flies over the city, he feels a sharp pain in his heart. He gets very upset when children bully each other.

Today, Kayden says he is tired of the bully calling him names and making fun of his sister.
He is going to let the bully know he is not to bother them again.
"We both need some confidence to stand up to the bully," Tayden says.
"Where can we get confidence from?" asks Kayden.
As the twins look puzzled, Captain Confidence sprinkles the seeds of confidence on them.

The twins walk to the corner where the bully awaits and start running toward him. The bully looks startled and starts to walk backward in fear. Kayden and Tayden scream at the bully to leave them alone and to never make fun of them again. The bully is scared and starts to cry.

"I'm sorry, I just wanted to be your friend, but I didn't know how to be a friend with you two," the bully says.

"Can you teach me how to be confident?" asks the bully.
Kayden and Tayden smile and speak at the same time. "Yes, because confidence is everything."

Captain Confidence saves the day!